How to Hide a Lion at School

ALISON GREEN BOOKS

Helen Stephens

Iris and her lion went everywhere together.

The lion was the town hero, because he once rescued the mayor's best candlesticks from some robbers.

But there was one place where they couldn't go together – and that was school. Iris's teacher, Miss Holland, said lions weren't allowed at school.

SCHOOL LANE

The lion didn't want to be apart from Iris, though, so every day he'd sneak after her.

But no matter
where the lion hid . . .

behind the whiteboard,

inside the piano,

behind the children's coats ...

Miss Holland always found him.
"I've got eyes at the back of my head," she'd say.
And she'd send him home.

But one day, instead of going straight home, the lion thought he'd have a nap in a nice sunny spot outside the school, so he could still hear the children playing in the playground.

Welcome to TWEEDMOUTH SCHOOL

But his nice sunny spot was actually a bus.

BUS

And the children weren't going out to play today . . .

. . . they were going on a school trip!
Nobody noticed the sleeping lion as they got on the bus.

And the lion was very surprised when he woke up.

What was happening?
And where was he going?

The bus pulled up outside a big building,
and all of the children trooped out.
The lion waited till they'd
all gone in . . .

. . . and then he sneaked in after them.

He found lots of good places to hide.

First he hid in a clock.

Then he hid in an aeroplane.

And then he hid in a suit of armour.

But then they came to the ancient Egypt room
– and that's where Iris spotted him.

"Oh, no!" said Iris. "Miss Holland will see you!
We'll have to find you a better place to hide."
Luckily, everyone was going to the loo, and that gave Iris an idea.

She fetched as many toilet rolls as she could carry, and wrapped the lion up like an Egyptian mummy.

It was a perfect disguise . . .

... until an old lady walked past with a tickly nose.

"A-a-a-tishoo!"

sneezed the old lady.

"A tissue?" thought the lion, and he handed her the end of one of his toilet rolls. "Thank you! How handy," said the old lady. "I just need a little bit more ..."

But as she tugged at the paper, the lion unravelled!

"A lion!" screamed the old lady. "He'll eat us all!"

"He's not that kind of lion," said Iris.

MUSEUM TICKETS

But the security guards ordered
him out of the museum just the same.
Miss Holland looked very cross, too.

The lion found a hiding place outside and waited till the children trooped back to the bus.

Then he hitched a lift on a lorry behind them. It was very windy and rainy, and the lion had to hold on tight.

The wind blew harder.
It blew the leaves off the trees.

Then it blew the twigs off the branches.

And then it blew over...

CRAASH!

The bus screeched to a halt. The whole road was blocked!

"Well, this bus isn't going anywhere," said the driver.
"But how will we get back to school?" said Miss Holland.
It was wet and windy and far too far to walk.

The lion looked at them anxiously.
The children looked very tired and cold.
He knew Miss Holland was cross with
him, but he had to go and help. So
he tiptoed down from the lorry.

"Not that lion again!"
said Miss Holland.
"But he's come to rescue us!"
said Iris. "We just need to
climb on his back."

They all held on tight — even Miss Holland.
Then with one huge leap, the lion jumped
right over the fallen tree.

Then the lion carried them all the way through the town and back to school. The townspeople clapped and cheered.

"What a kind lion," said Miss Holland. "I always said so."

And from that day on, the class never used the school bus again.
They always travelled . . .

. . . by lion!

"You're much better than a bus,"
said Iris.

For teachers everywhere, who
tackle a new adventure every day

First published in the UK in 2016 by
Alison Green Books
An imprint of Scholastic Children's Books
Euston House, 24 Eversholt Street
London NW1 1DB, UK
A division of Scholastic Ltd
www.scholastic.co.uk
London – New York – Toronto – Sydney – Auckland
Mexico City – New Delhi – Hong Kong

Copyright © 2016 Helen Stephens

HB ISBN: 978 1 407166 30 8
PB ISBN: 978 1 407166 31 5

10 9 8 7 6 5 4 3

The moral rights of Helen Stephens have been asserted.

Papers used by Scholastic Children's Books are made
from wood grown in sustainable forests.